IFWG Publishing's
Chapbook line of titles

Black Moon: Graphic Speculative Flash Fiction, by Eugen Bacon

Tool Tales: Microfifiction Inspired by Antique Tools, by Kaaron Warren (photography by Elen Datlow)

Stark Naked (poetry collection) by Silvia Cantón Rondoni

Infectious Hope: Poems of Hope and Resilience From the Pandemic, edited by Silvia Cantón Rondoni

Morace's Story (children's novella, companion to Walking the Tree) by Kaaron Warren

Songs From a White Heart (poetry collection), by Jack Dann

Sunset Tales: Haunting Tales of Africa, by Biola Olatunde

Sunset Tales

Tales

Haunted Tales of Africa

Biola Olatunde

Sunset Tales: Haunted Tales of Africa

All Rights Reserved

ISBN-13: 978-1-925496-33-8

Copyright ©2023 Biola Olatunde
V1.0 Second Edition

First Published 2014
by IFWG Publishing

Printed in Garamond and Cleaver's Juvenia Heavy typefaces.

IFWG Publishing International
Melbourne

www.ifwgpublishing.com

TABLE OF CONTENTS

Publisher's Introduction

In July 2021 Biola Olatunde, a much-loved and prolific writer for IFWG Publishing, passed away. Because she lived in Nigeria, and the intermittent times we communicated, I didn't find out about this event until February 2022. I was shocked. She was 70 years old and was way too young to die. It took a lot of time to process this information.

Prior to Biola passing we had agreed to publish a chapbook of her poetry in 2023—while we have had the pleasure and privilege to publish four of her novels, we knew that her particular strengths were poetry and screenplay writing. We wanted her poetry. Unfortunately, if she had written any poetry for this project they are now lost. It took over six months to come to this realisation and we were disappointed. We wanted to find a long-lasting way to pay respect to Biola's memory.

Some years ago IFWG published a series of ebook-only 'chapbooks' with some modest success. One of these was a collection of six short stories by Biola called 'Sunset Tales'. It didn't take long for us to decide to republish it, in a second-editon form, in our chapbook print series. We wanted to get it right, and do it right for Biola. This book you are holding in your hands is the culmination of this process.

I wish to thank Sarah Heard for her special effort to sensitively edit the original manuscript, Greg Chapman for his art and design work for the cover, and Tony Olatunde for allowing us to publish this second edition.

You now know the background, but I want to write a few more words about Biola. She had a spirit the size of Africa and had amazing creative energy. I know she had, at times, struggled with financial and cultural issues in modern-day Nigeria, but her contagious smile prevaled, and was always excited to see her work published by our company. There were nights (my time) when we would have long chats through various internet apps and it was almost like I was sitting opposite her with our favourite beverages in hand. For many years I called her my 'African sister'—and I meant it. I still do.

Being a small publisher, and smaller still when we published Biola's novels, we didn't get the sales she deserved. It was tougher still trying to sell her books in Nigeria. Nevertheless, she was over the moon to have published through us and this does warm my heart. *Sunset Tales: Haunting Tales of Africa*, is our last opportunity to publish Biola again, and I am sure she would have cried out with joy.

This thought alone makes this exercise worth it.

Ake, Biola.

Gerry Huntman
Managing Director, IFWG Publishing
Gold Coast, Australia
January 2023

BEFORE GRANDMA DIED

She stood in front of the mirror and gave herself a hard look. She searched the old face, not particularly shocked with the amount of gray that had increased from the last time she looked at herself this way. She noted the creases in the corners of her mouth and her chin. The skin was beginning to give way. It had been some six months now and she was expecting to see a difference. *Maybe it should be my teeth,* she thought, and she bared them for close inspection. No signs of fangs yet. They still looked old, decaying, and yes, one tooth less from years ago when he had punched her in the face.

How was she to look now? Tears formed like dark pools in her tired eyes and the silence around her was deafening. She went through the routine again, a routine that had become a form of ritual.

Her phone was a part of the routine. She performed a ritual with it every morning after her body inspection, since the day she died within—the day when she watched in horror, aghast as her heart was stabbed and love bled out of her.

In the deafening silence, she felt the blows again and again. The horrible pronouncement as she descended deep into an abyss, and darkness enveloped her, when her daughter screamed the terrible words.

"You frigging bloody witch!"

In her tribe and tradition it was the heaviest indictment a woman could receive.

The knife twisted again and the world stopped breathing. From a distance, as the blood flowed, she did not feel the thrusts again even as she heard the words pounding away at her heart and tearing it into shreds.

She felt herself shiver with remembrance of her blinding rage when she held her daughter by the throat in a desperate denial that she had not actually heard the words nor felt the blows. Her heart threatened to give way again so she gulped and moved away.

The joys of motherhood mocked her, as she relentlessly tried again to remember how it all started.

The pronouncement had been made in the open, in full hearing of anyone passing (there were two women who stood and stared), then, oh yes, there was her neighbor who lived in the next flat (they hardly ever talked), who also glared in witness.

Disgrace and pronouncement complete and…oh, she remembered just in time, it was her housekeeper's day, so the housekeeper had tried to pull them apart, or, more correctly, pull her away from the beating.

"You frigging bloody witch!"

She died.

Six months later, still in the dark tomb of unending misery and bleeding heart, she stood and stared at the mirror each morning. She had formed the habit of having three baths every morning, one in the afternoon, and two at night. She slept alone, wrapped like a cocoon in the warm misery and tears. She inspected her teeth every morning as she wanted to be the first to notice the fangs. She remembered that witches were expected to have birds in their stomachs so she ate sparingly hoping to starve whatever bird was in there, and kept away from anyone in case they heard her rumbling stomach.

She also stared at her phone. It had not rung in six months. She always bought phone credits and played the expected reunion back in her mind. *How long is the conversation going to be?* Love restored and she would be accepted as a mother again.

She remembered the silent walks she made at night so no one will see her. Nobody should see her silent vigil along the road to her daughter's house where she watched the lights and heard the laughter of her grandchildren. She particularly missed her granddaughter: her cheerful smile, the warmth as she nestled close showing the stories she had written at school.

Her heart started bleeding again and she sighed. Worse was to come as she moved away from the mirror, remembering the night when she had reached her guard post and saw the place completely dark. No lights, no voices, and the windows were bare as the wind screamed a mockery, "*You bloody frigging witch!*"

She was bathed in icy cold terror throughout that night.

A neighbor told her that the occupants had moved during the day. She staggered home, exhausted, and too tired to even inspect the pain. She spent the whole day staring at the phone, willing it to ring, and she prayed for release from the pain.

She also prayed for release—to walk away from a daughter she had brought alone into the world, had watched over, slaved to send to school, and who one day six months ago had beaten her and called her a witch. In a small whisper from a dried-up throat, she had kept asking why.

"*Because I asked when you will return money you took from my small business that had kept us alive from hunger.*"

She had waited all these months for the terrible words to be retracted, an explanation that the beating and denouncement had been a momentary madness. She had dreaded the visit of the elders if they should ask her to visit the palace, and lived terrified of the glances of friends and neighbors alike.

"*You bloody frigging witch!*"

She was too terrified by the pronouncement to even ask why, for in all her nightmares she had only been guilty of love.

Then the phone rang endlessly.

We opened the door.

Grandma was dead.

Court Is
In Session

A friend invited me once to attend a court session. He was trying to reassure me that there was nothing to be afraid about our judicial system. I had nothing to do for that day and did not feel like working on the computer, so I walked over from my office to the court, which was some distance away.

It was packed already. A young man was in the dock for killing his mum. His eyes were haunted and strained. You could tell he was under great stress. His wife and members of his family were sitting huddled together and everyone stared at the judge.

One lady sat quietly. She was not agitated, nor was she crying. She was dressed simply and elegantly almost like the judge herself. Her gray hair indicated she was most likely in her sixties. I was intrigued by her self-restraint.

I'd seen a couple of white garmented prophets outside the church assuring the relatives that they had nothing to worry about. I asked my friend why the boy—actually, the young man—was charged with killing his mother. He whispered back that he had deliberately driven his mother over the edge of cliff with his car because he had accused her of witchcraft.

"Hmm, who fingered her as a witch?" I asked my friend, darkly amused.

He indicated the white garmented prophets outside the court premises.

I groaned and craned my neck to get a better view of the court. I noticed a few of my journalist friends were intrigued by the story and had come to watch the proceedings. I wondered what the elegant lady was doing so I murmured an excuse to my friend and went over to sit beside her.

She gave me a cursory glance and I had a vision of a very beautiful, graceful old lady. She sat still, calmly watching.

I tried to start a quiet conversation. "You know the young man being charged?"

"I think so, since he was born actually," she said with a smile.

"I see, you must be feeling bad about this then," I said.

She turned and gave me a calm glance through clear brown eyes, and, with a slight graceful nod of her head, indicated the young man at the dock. "His relatives have been praying and asking that the Almighty come to their aid, but I wonder if He is listening."

I shrugged, "I am sorry but I'm—"

"Not into religion, I know that," she finished for me, with a slight smile.

"Have you ever wondered why God has never seen fit to kill the Devil? I mean that would save a lot of misery. The misery of a religion and the bottomless stupidity we inflict on ourselves."

We were silent as the judge walked in and started reading her judgment. My companion listened impassively.

The judge had declared the case a non-issue ordering a re-trial for manslaughter.

The court erupted into loud jubilation. My old lady stood

up. She was not smiling nor was she upset; just calm.

I commented that at least she would be relieved to know it had come out well for the young man. She simply inclined her head. I was now really interested in talking to her further so I asked if I might call on her sometime.

She was amused at my request. "That could be a problem as I have just retired from active duty and I am kind of resting now. Just pay the occasional visit into the world, you know."

I remarked that she seemed to know me and so had the advantage.

She said she had often watched my programs and thought I was doing okay.

I pressed for her name and she smiled and gave me her hand.

"I used to be called Justice Anike Williams," she said, and smiling, left.

I went over to my friend and told him about the old lady. He listened as we walked out the court but almost crashed the car at the fence when I mentioned the name of the lady I had been talking to.

"You could have killed us!" I complained.

He stared at me. "Are you sure of the name of the lady you talked to?" he asked.

"Yes, of course. I just told you," I snapped, checking to see if I had any injuries.

I went cold, however, with his next comment. "Justice Anike Williams is the mother of the young man just acquitted and she died in that accident two years ago. I attended the funeral. Who exactly have you been talking to?"

DREAM
MURDER

He did not want to go home. He stared at the table in front of him as the shadows gathered, the hustle of the city slowing down as the night hawkers set up. He sat quietly as the sounds around him changed in tone and volume. *Why bother going home?* he asked himself. *Should I go to the police? And tell them what?* He shuddered and slouched deeper into his chair. At least he should make some attempt to put on the light. *I can always go see the pastor,* he told himself, *or one of these miracle churches where they would promise me release… from? My wife?*

No pastor; it is not about divorce. She is giving me everything I ask for. Good food every time I ask for it. Right figure, you know the type of figure that seems to have—no don't even think about it.

His skin crawled and he knew he was afraid. Should he tell his mum? "I told you she was the wrong color, didn't I?" his mother would scream at him, and then suggest they go ask the ancient one, or she would suggest a village wife as an antidote.

What would he tell the police? They had seen worse maybe. So his story wouldn't be anything new—except maybe raise a laugh.

Was he really frightened? He really didn't believe that, did he? But then, did he dare to say it to her? He also felt jealous. She had described the affair with such detail he was not so sure he should not actually head for the divorce courts. *I should give Ade a call.* He imagined Ade's smile and he cringed, for he also remembered that his friend had been skeptical when he had come in excited that he was going to marry Kike.

He tried to remember that party Kike told him about. She had acted like a normal lady. You know, a quiet, respectable, married lady. As always, she had not said much either, just kept to her corner and stayed close to him. What was the conversation at that party? Not much—er, okay, yes, he remembered. Jide had come over. Did he notice anything in the handshake he gave his wife? Jide, bland Jide, who they all teased because he never seemed interested in women. He looked and acted as if he was happily married.

How was I to know the man was a raging lover or, at least, her dream lover? I'm going crazy. But what the hell was the man doing in the dreams of his wife?

That is right, he mocked himself. Was he to report to the police that his wife was having an affair with a man in her dreams?

He was not going to give the same reason to Ade that he wanted to divorce his wife because she had a lover in her dreams and had been dumb enough to tell him.

He shifted in the chair, knowing he was afraid to admit to what had frightened him was not the explicit lovemaking she had described but what had happened.

"I hit him in the head with a stick and he called me the next day to say he had a headache. Why is he having the same dream as me, and why is he having a headache when I only hit him in the dream?"

He had stared at her as she asked that question, her

eyes wide and worried, tears filling them as she gave the final installment to the story. He could not ask her if she had enjoyed the lovemaking in the dream, or if Jide was better than him. He swore at himself in self-pity.

"I warned him not to bother me again because next time I wouldn't just hit him with a stick, I would come with a knife and stick it up and kill him," were her final words, and he remembered how he had backed away. The phone call to Jide, how his throat went dry when it was picked up by a stranger who said Jide was found dead in his bed with blood on his lips.

He came to work in a daze.

It was not the dream lover, but his wife. He was afraid to go home because he was afraid of his wife. *Go home to your loving wife,* he told himself, and the phone rang with the special ringtone he had allocated to her. He jerked as if he had been stung and stared at the phone.

He searched in the drawer for the bottle of whisky and took a shot. He did not feel better. *I mean, if I am going to die, I had better do it like a man.* Had she marked him too? He heard that such people do not like eating bitter meat, and he shuddered.

The phone rang again; it was his wife calling.

The janitor knocked on the door as he crashed to the floor.

He could not tell when he got home, but he remembered waking up in the middle of the night to pee. His wife slept peacefully beside him. There was no point telling her that just thinking of her had caused him to faint in the office. He shrugged, and, still sleepy, turned over and tried to pull the coverlet over him. When he heard a deep sarcastic laughter, he sat up in sheer terror.

There was no one else in the room yet he was prepared to swear that a male voice had just laughed. He rubbed his eyes and snapped on the bedside lamp. The room was peaceful, his wife, Kike, was sleeping peacefully, curled up and facing him. He studied her face and wondered why he was so frightened of her. *She is just as frightened as I am.* But he still turned away and resolutely closed his eyes. *Maybe I really should think of going to church more often.*

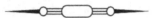

Things quietened down for a few days and Bode felt peace return to his heart. He even took Kike out on a lunch date a week later and, that was when Arike walked up to their table. Bode was pleased to see her and happily introduced Kike to Arike. Kike invited her to join their table and all three shared lunch making jokes and generally having a good time.

Two days later, Arike paid a surprise call at his office and they chatted.

"You look radiant," Bode observed, as he gave Arike a smiling once over. They had always been friends and colleagues. Arike had been promoted to business manager of their bank and was transferred North to Kaduna when the bank merged with another. Kike used to tease that Arike was a better financial expert than him and she would laugh and shrug at fate.

Arike got married six months ago to Kole, his best friend, who worked for Fortune Oil and Gas. Kole and Arike were properly introduced to each other at his wedding.

"How is my best friend?" Bode asked now.

"Fine, I think."

"Don't you know?"

"I left him in Port Harcourt two weeks ago."

"Yikes, he is back in that hell hole of kidnappers?"

"It is the oil city and money literally flows on the streets," Arike said, laughing.

"No wonder you look so wonderful, you have been spending my friend's money."

Arike laughed again and pulled her chair close. "I have a question for you."

"Yeah?"

"What is wrong with Kike?"

Bode clenched his hands under the table, but his expression remained genial. "Wrong? How?"

"Something is wrong and I can sense it."

Bode looked out the window to gain time for his emotions to stay under control then noticed Arike shaking her head. "I really have no idea what you are talking about. What do you mean?"

Arike sighed. "Well something doesn't seem right but I can't put a finger on it. I just feel something."

Bode smiled and pretended to be highly amused. "You women are always searching for things that do not exist except in your pretty heads."

Arike laughed. "I know one thing that definitely exists. Kole and I are expecting a baby."

"Wow! Congratulations! When?"

"Hey, whoa, hold your horses, I haven't told your friend yet—just coming from the doctor for the confirmation. Think you can come over for dinner tomorrow night? He will be in town a few hours from now. He's on the two o'clock flight, so I am telling him tonight. As his best friend, I wanted to let you know; besides I can't keep such news to myself. You are going to be godfather by the way."

Bode laughed and opened his drawer, then closed it again. "You are not going to be drinking alcohol now are you?"

"Bode! The pregnancy is only six weeks old. I don't feel any symptoms. A glass of wine would be harmless."

They shared a glass and chatted over clients, the office, and eventually Arike left.

Bode drove home in a happy exhilarated mood, and on entering their home, instinctively gave his wife a hug and kiss.

Kike sniffed and wrinkled her brows. "I can smell pregnancy around—have you been talking with a pregnant client? The smell of a fetus is strong on you."

There was stunned silence as Bode's jaw dropped in shock.

They both stared at each other in mutual horror as Bode slowly collapsed in a chair, shivering with dread.

THE
BATS

The conversation appeared to go on forever. He kept looking at his watch hoping the guys would make up their minds and he could get out of the office. It seemed like he had been there for hours. The Managing Director came to a decision and Dimeji snapped his mind to the present as he heard the man cough, fixing a decisive expression on his face.

"I think we can agree that you would do the program for us for three million. We think we can manage that."

Dimeji shook his head and stood up, "I will accept four, Mr. Richards, that is a fair price."

The man gave him a keen glance and grinned. "Let's make it three and half—the rest of the Board are going to kill me but what the hell, it is my skin they will roast." He outstretched his hands.

Dimeji shook hands and the deal was concluded.

When he stepped out of the air-conditioned office into the main street, he switched on his phone. He walked briskly to where his car was packed, sighing at the gathering bedlam of automobiles, blaring horns, and the mass of pedestrians that came at him in waves. His mind sank at the thought of driving through the crazy traffic, but he shrugged and walked towards his car.

The call came and he sighed, wondering if he ought to pick up the call. He was close to his car. Besides, from the corner of his eye he had seen the *Area Boys*—those street touts were terrorists of a kind and people generally avoided them. They were a menace and could frustrate unsuspecting pedestrians. Dimeji did not want their attention or attract it by answering his phone. So he briskly walked to the car park hoping whoever was calling would call back and he could answer in the safety of his car.

He was tired and moved quickly, easing his car into the gridlock of the evening traffic. Apart from the menace of the Area Boys, there was the need to be careful as the *Lastma* boys were still around, intent on making last minute pickings on motorists over any traffic offence, real or imagined. These traffic personnel were simply called *Lastma*. He sighed and followed the traffic.

A flurry behind him made him jump. *A bat!* His skin suddenly crawled and a scream died abruptly in his throat as he shooed the darn thing out of his car, avoiding hitting the trailer in front of him by bare inches. *What the hell. How had that gotten into a closed car?* He was more angry than frightened.

He sighed as he saw long lines of car lights far into the horizon. It was going to be one of those nights. His phone rang. *Abike calling,* said his phone.

A smile tugged at his lips as he answered to the throaty deep voice of his wife. It was crazy the way her voice always gave him a hard on. *Almost instantly,* he often said to himself. Their relationship never made sense, to him or to anyone who had known them for all the time they have been together.

He chuckled as he replied to her query about if he was close to her friend's house yet. "Not likely until maybe midnight. I am in Lagos, remember? It is bedlam here right now."

She laughed making him adjust his trousers. He wanted to be in bed with her right then and she picked up that desire in his voice, laughing. They chatted for a while and he promised to call when he arrived at her friend's home. He turned the handset off and tried the best he could to concentrate on the traffic.

Another bat flew across his windscreen almost causing him to bump into the car in front, but he braked just in time, swearing, hastily increasing the air conditioning in the car. He hated Lagos and hated driving at night even more. He also was not so sure he actually wanted to spend the night in Lara's home, but he had promised Abike that he would. *But where did all the bats come from?* he wondered absently, as he followed the traffic and avoided the *danfo* buses as well as the tricycles that defied all control squeezing into every space they can. There were the infernal *okada* riders as well. Adding to all his misery, pedestrians were crossing and hawking all manner of wares, and the roadside musicians, records shops and—*blast!*—the religious revivalists were everywhere. He wondered why anybody in his or her right mind would like to live in Lagos. It was like living in bedlam. His mother never understood why he was always in a hurry to return to the quiet unhurried life of Akure.

Dimeji's mind wandered as he drove at the snail pace of the traffic. He had been born in Lagos, left from there to London in the tradition of his age mates, got his degree, worked for a further five years, and decided to come home so he could discuss his wedding plans with his family. That was the plan, and that was ten years ago. He never returned to London.

It was just a trip to one of the towns outside Lagos to see his aunt, who was to represent his mother at his wedding, and pick the mandatory *aso oke*.

He had stood outside her house the morning after his arrival as Abike walked past. One minute he had been chatting with his Aunty, when his voice trailed off as he suddenly found himself breathing hard and desperately praying that the lady walking past would stop or look at him. She walked right over to him to say hello to his Aunty. He tried very hard to this day to remember what he had been saying but he never could. He recalled, however, walking over and smiling and she looked at him and he was lost.

His next words shocked everybody including himself, "Please marry me."

The silence was thick as they all stared at him and she spoke in that deep voice that was so masculine in a face that was totally feminine, "I beg your pardon?"

His Aunty had simply stared and cleared her throat, frowning heavily at him in reproach. Her voice was sharp as she told her friend that her nephew had come to finalize his wedding plans and maybe he was still reliving the way he had proposed.

Abike had smiled in understanding and, not giving him a second glance, went on her way. Alarmed, he hurried after her insisting he meant every word he said.

Dimeji smiled now as his mind replayed the panic, tears, and total chaos of the first seven months after that first day. He wrote a long letter to Jane calling off the wedding—*her* wedding, he stressed. His mother made a panicked, hurried trip to Akure following his announcement in a vain effort to appeal to Abike to release him from the enchanted spell placed on him.

Dimeji refused to even return to Lagos. He sent his letter of resignation to his office in London. His mother called for other relatives to help. They were sure he was under a very powerful spell. Prayer warriors were drafted to help out in breaking the enchantment.

Each time any of his relatives came to see Abike, she was cool, remote, and exhibited controlled anger, asking everyone to leave her house each time they came. Dimeji, however, refused to leave. He couldn't. He begged, cried, and explained—at least he tried to explain—what was wrong with him, but he did not know it himself. They took him to all the prayer houses seeking solutions for his instant and almost total captivation. Nobody could shake him. He was adamant. He wanted to marry Abike, full stop.

It was like an obsession. Abike would cry helplessly begging him to go and he couldn't. He was as helpless as she was. No, he corrected himself, she was never helpless; just bemused, wondering what she had ever done to attract "such pestilence", she would say. Dimeji smiled and insisted, pled, and bore the brunt of the wails, screams and abuse of his mother.

It was his brother Akin who solved the problem with-out meaning to. The family sent for him to come to the aid of the family from far away Ikom, a border town with Cameroon. His brother lived in Cross River State and made the nine-hour grueling journey on bad roads, surviving armed robbers along the way to come and sort his kid brother out. Dimeji remembered he was in Abike's office trying to persuade her to come for lunch when his brother barged in. All three stared at each other. Abike, who had angrily been telling him to push off had stared in the same anger at his brother, asked Akin who he wanted to see.

His brother simply sat at the table and offered to pay for the lunch if he can come as well. Dimeji still laughed at how his brother had lost the battle to save him without much of a fight, or even a raised voice.

A very sheepish Akin had asked him what story he was to tell his expectantly waiting mother when he returned to Lagos. Dimeji laughed, stating it was the Abike effect.

Five people attended his wedding three months later: his friend, Taju, who had been summoned to come to Nigeria from America, his cousin, and the besotted Akin, his older brother. Abike came with her Chinese friend Lin. It was a very strange wedding as Abike returned to work almost immediately. Peace was made within a year and a daughter later with the rest of the family. Gradually the extended family had accepted that Dimeji had truly fallen in love. After all, spells usually last only seven years they had reasoned. Dimeji and Abike had been married for ten.

Two daughters came in quick succession and Dimeji's mother was now a firm fan of Abike and would start practically every sentence with, "Abike thinks…"

All seemed well until Abike introduced her friend Lara to him. Lara had been living in London with her husband when Abike got married and so Dimeji never met her until two years ago. His skin crawled, his hands went clammy, and he had struggled to maintain a smile when they met for the first time. Dimeji felt Lara was ugly and there was a sense of the sinister about her.

That first night in the home of Lara, he had been unable to sleep. Lara had spent hours talking to Abike, so maybe that was why he had been uneasy. But then he saw the bats. *No, not in the room, but just outside the guest room windows.*

He mentioned the bats to Abike and she said airily that the bats were nature's joke in combining a bird with a mammal. She had calmed him down. But he could not sleep. He was happy that they left Lagos the next day. However, for a few more nights, he kept dreaming of bats. They flapped in his dreams and chattered endlessly. It affected his work.

One morning, about a week after their return from Lagos, he held his wife, breathed in her warmth, when he suddenly heard the bats again. He jerked his head and listened. Abike asked him what the matter was and he had shrugged saying he just remembered something.

He decided to visit his friend Taju who was back in Nigeria. He explained about the bats and Taju had laughed that he did not think it meant anything, but just to be sure they went to visit Baba Aladura at Ketu. A fruit fast was recommended for him. Baba took him to a stream on the seventh day and he felt cleansed and invigorated. Nothing happened after that and he went back to his normal schedule.

Dimeji did not know why he was getting all these recoll- ections as the traffic eased and he made better progress to Lara's home. He drove in. The house was palatial and Lara descended the stairs in a flowing, almost see-through long dress, reeking of perfume and jangling with bracelets. She hugged him and said, "You survived the traffic I can see. I was on the phone with Abike. I guess I had better tell her you are safely here. She kept checking every five minutes, I swear."

Dimeji said he had already called his wife the minute

he drove in. A tiny frown came into Lara's face but she still smiled and called her housekeeper to get her guest dinner. Lara mentioned that a guest room was ready for him. She appeared to be amused about something.

Dinner did not take long and he retired to the guest room for a shower when he saw the first bat. He froze as the hair on the back of his neck rose, and his skin erupted in goosebumps.

"Ergh," he said to himself, swatting at the bat as it flew out of the room. He fastened the windows shut and switched on the air conditioning.

His phone rang, it was Abike.

"The bats are back, darling," he blurted, and chagrined. He sounded like a frightened boy. So he laughed and tried to joke, but found he was sweating and his hands were shaking.

"Bats? What bats, sweetheart? There are bats in the room?" Abike asked anxiously.

"Er...well, I just chased one out," he tried to say in a casual voice, but he felt his rising fear again.

Abike sighed over the phone, "I am sorry, love, it is Lara, I guess, with those silly trees too close to the house and they do tend to attract bats. I told her that several times, but I think she enjoys the conversation of the bats."

"She understands what the bats are saying"? Dimeji queried, his voice rising an octave and his skin goosebumping again.

"Well she claims she does. She just likes being spooky. Ask her to change your room. She has more than one guest room; you don't have to sleep in a bat room, love."

Dimeji swallowed and tried to speak in a casual and calm voice, even as he felt his heartbeat race. "I guess it's nothing much, I just don't like bats you know and, well, it is just one night. Will leave as early as I can in the morning. Should I pick you up at the office?"

"That will be fine. I have that advert meeting for twelve. Would be nice if you come in time to sit in so they don't give me a price and I say yes too quickly, right?"

He laughed, kissed her through the phone, and had a bath. He chided himself for being nervous about bats and settled in for the night.

Much later, the whispering voices woke him and he sat up with a start. He had been having a silly dream in which…he pulled his mind away from the dream. He did not feel like repeating it to himself. He had been making love to his wife or some figure he had assumed was his wife, but he had felt bony flesh and not the warm softness of Abike, and he could almost swear that he saw the ends of a flowing gown as it swished over him.

He was also sweating, so he turned on the bedside light and gasped. There were two bats in the room. *How did they enter?*

A soft knock sounded on the door and he froze. Someone tried very gently to open the door and Dimeji searched the room for anything strong enough to defend himself.

The bats kept up their chatter just by the window and the door was tried again. He went to the door trying to determine who it was. Just soft scratching noises—his heart pounded. *Armed robbers?* The house was silent. In the distance, a night guard struck a gong twice. It meant it was 2 am. *If they are armed robbers they would not be so silent*, he thought to himself. He silently went to the window and softly tried to open it. The curtains billowed out indicating that someone sometime in the night had already opened them. He closed them by the soft light of the bed.

He heard a soft click as he tiptoed to the bathroom, leaving the door slightly open, giving himself the opportunity to see robbers if his room was invaded.

He grabbed the toilet seat as a strong urge to pee gripped him. The door opened and the intruder walked in, surprised to see the bed light on.

From his concealment in the bathroom, Dimeji was shocked. Standing in the middle of the bedroom was Lara with no clothes on. She looked unearthly and bony, and disgust rose in him. Dimeji dashed back to the toilet and made peeing sounds and flushed the toilet noisily. His bedroom door closed. There was nobody in the bedroom after he had given her a decent five minutes to leave.

Dimeji sat on the bed and laughed till tears rolled down his cheeks. He kept watch on the door for the rest of the night as all types of thoughts assailed him. He had heard stories of certain women using the semen of men for money-making purposes. They usually made love to such men, placing them under a spell. Dimeji knew that such men became slaves to those women and all their intended wealth would be appropriated. Such men would lose weight as the wealth of the women increased.

Dimeji left as early as he could the next morning knowing he could not mention his experience to Abike. Lara returned to London the following week and Abike kept wondering at the sudden departure, but Dimeji always had a smile, a knowing look, but no comments. He never saw the bats again.

THE DEVIL
LAUGHED

Sometimes you try to laugh in an effort to push far away the despair eating at you. My mother used to say, "What can't talk should not be able to defeat you." I sit for hours staring at the blank screen. Not because I don't have anything to say but I'm swamped by what I need to say, and wonder why I should bother saying it. It is just another twenty-four hours anyway. Another day to live through.

The vendor calls and I shrug, not because the news is nothing but because I am scared to learn I have ceased to exist as Nigerian, never mind the fact that I am not even sure of my chances to live as a human being. I am like every person I know: I want an identity, a country, a home, and a love.

It is not too much to ask for this for yourself angrily and then sigh as depression, like some stone, settles in the pit of your stomach. I am reviled by people from other countries that wonder what I think I am being, who I am, and being from that place of the earth that has been damned and condemned.

Anger slowly boils like a cauldron and I feebly attempt to pour ice into it. I count to ten before I speak so that the pain should not spill out from my guts.

I am done being angry. It has fed me for so long only I found that I'm still very hungry, so I reluctantly accept that the anger has not done much…and then I listen…to the painful thud of my heart as it hides itself away from me.

Three hundred and sixty-five days of watching for an opportunity to make good. I am desperate as first there is anger from the children, and then I shrivel as I see the wrath slowly turns to contempt. It is the worst indictment you could possibly endure. Love like some measly cancer has settled in my soul and won't let go even as I feel the rejection from hungry puzzled faces and their questions.

"You lost as a parent," the voice cackles at me, and I feel the lash as I grit my teeth and plod the streets looking for the opportunity to earn bread for another wasted twenty-four hours. The door opens and the children look up; my wife turns over and faces the door. The expectant faces drop to boredom and my heart sinks.

"Oh, it's you," they say with the least interest in what I have to offer.

The other day I had stared for long hours at the ocean wondering if the fishes in it might find my body acceptable as a meal. "It will be too bony and not rich enough," the infernal taunting voice says close to my ears and I feel my heart crying. A sob escapes and I am alarmed, checking if anyone heard my miserable sob.

Someone is playing, 'I am black and proud', and I snort.

It is the first hint of healthy anger I have heard or felt in a long while. The landlord has a letter for me: "Sir, my nephew will be returning from his studies abroad and we would need your room for him to stay while he starts on his job with the Apex Bank". *Hmmm, the shark is even willing to forgo his eighteen months rent arrears…hmmm…but where are you going?*

No place, not even hell since the voice said I do not even have a vacant room there. Not even standing space.

"You see we have so many applicants, those egg heads who have robbed the country blind, oil subsidy thieves, the ones who collected thousands of dollars to catch another thief and said he only collected money and not bribes. Honestly, the Devil holds those guys in deep admiration. There are some escapades he never could have dreamed of. We are planning a royal reception for them."

"Then there is the new fashion of religion by death, you know, a few bombs here and there and our colleague is laughing. He has so frightened you all into a stupor. When I told the Boss about your request about jumping into the ocean he snorted and said you ought to have your head examined. I did that and found nothing there."

I collapsed on the torn mattress. A rat scurried away from my feet and I made an attempt to kill it as a fierce hunger for meat grabbed me. I was so weak from all the walking and hunger that I stumbled and the rat escaped, snorting. A man should not be this hopeless and helpless. Even I was beginning to hold myself in contempt.

The door opened and my wife came in and stood arms akimbo, watching me. I stared back helplessly and suddenly broke down and wept, asking her to please take the children and leave.

She said nothing and left.

I staggered around the room, dazed, and finally collapsed into a chair.

I closed my eyes and dreamt of food. I even smelt the aroma. Someone was shaking me, trying to make me open my eyes and I struggled to comply. She looked at me and smiled. I blinked. *Okay, I must have died. Devil changed his mind and gave me a room.*

The children came in and lined themselves against the wall.

"What? You died too?" I asked, pointing my fingers at them, and I started trembling. "Oh Lord, not them too. I am sorry."

"Really?"

"Yes, please, just me should be enough."

"They are coming along with us and stop sniveling," the sharp voice retorted.

What?

I became conscious of my real state and the packed bags.

"We are leaving for the village; I got you a job as the headmaster of your old school. You will resume next week. You can still teach, can't you? Remember all those fiery speeches, the applause as the students came back to thank you for showing them how to be a man. Well one of your students met me in the street and we talked about you. He did not think it was right for you to stop teaching. He said it was destiny, that is what Paul said. Remember him? The skinny one who always never had enough to eat and he would come to our living room and you would sneak him money and paid his final exam fees? Well, he is a minister now; his convoy almost knocked me down. He recognized me and asked after you. You are going back to teaching and giving back dreams to young minds like him. You are not going to say no, are you?"

As I packed the papers on my fine wooden table, the memories came and I slowly sat back, considering my new office. The cackling voice had stopped but I still had hunger in my soul.

The door opened and my driver asked me if it was time to go home. I nodded and stood. It was just another twenty-four hours.

Yemoja's Client

He had a good reason to believe the stories his mother told him. This afternoon, as the sun beat on his bald pate and he felt the urge to go home, he remembered some of those stories. She had urged him to bring his first pay home.

"We will need to ask the gods to make the money yours," she had said with that anxious look about her person. Bode was not so sure he was ready to hand over all the money to a god who had taken its sweet time getting him a job.

Eight years of pounding the streets, scraping, and enduring insults, and by a freak chance, he got a job. Bode shifted in his seat and fixed a suspicious look on the priestess, wondering why he was feeling irritated and afraid. The irritation he understood, not the fear. *What did she mean, 'all the money'?* He definitely had no such intention. First of all, he was buying his mother that scarf she had wanted the last market day before he got the job. He was going to open an account and save some money for a decent coat. He also intended to fatten his skeletal frame to get some decent skin, not the wrinkled rag that wrapped his frame.

He dragged his mind to the room and shifted as he felt a trickle close to his crotch. He always sweated there

29

any time he was uncomfortable. He wondered if he should scratch the sweat and—

Her mild voice interrupted his thoughts again. "It is your mother's request that you ask the gods to bless your job and do something with your first pay."

That is it, he thought again, *do something with his money.* His mother had asked him to dip his hand in cold water when he was to receive his first pay. Bode had at first been amused and explained to her that the money would be paid into his bank (which he did not have at the time), and he would then need to apply for an ATM card. His mother looked at him and smiled. "The cash is given to you during one of these processes, right?"

"Yes," he replied, still mystified.

"Good. Just ensure you receive the money with a cold hand. I have appealed to Yemoja, the goddess of fortune, to ensure that the money stays cool in your hand and is not frittered by the wind. In fact, I asked the priestess to ensure that for you. She is expecting you tomorrow before you need to collect the money."

He gave the priestess a suspicious look. She returned his gaze with what he thought was a strange look—seconds later he understood the mischief. She asked him to undress and his jaw dropped. He stared wondering if he was asleep and going through a nightmare.

"Eh, I didn't quite get you. Did I hear you say I should undress?"

The priestess laughed. "I am giving you a spiritual wash, which means I have to dip you in the pool." She gave him a thorough once over look. "Nothing to get excited about, you know, you need a new skin as it is and food will do most of it, but you need to have a new skeleton maybe."

30

He tried to swallow his rage and found that he felt a personal shame that he was brought to this pass. *A graduate in quantum physics and I am groveling before a half-baked priestess.*

Bode took long seconds to calm down and uncurl his fists. He shook his head slowly to clear his mind and stood up. In a quiet voice he explained that he had no intention of undressing nor taking a dip in the cool puddle in front of him. *Oh Mother, not even for you.*

The priestess shrugged and handed him a piece of soap. "Go over to the back of the building and you will find a bathtub filled with water. It is in a covered shack, by the way, and you can dip with all your clothes on in the bathtub—would be interesting to see how you intend to get home in soggy clothes." She spoke in perfect cool English.

Bode's jaw dropped and he stared, but she had disappeared to the inner room with a quiet click indicating she had locked the door. Bode stood transfixed. *The priestess is educated.* A thousand thoughts rushed through his mind as he walked slowly to the back of the house to find, sure enough, that there was a bathtub, and everything was laid out as the priestess had said.

It was a chastened Bode that gave a timid knock minutes later when he had finished the bath. He felt like a fool and wondered how best to apologize for his crude behavior.

The priestess didn't seem to have noticed his new awkwardness but laid a hand on his chest and spoke a few words silently, then she touched his head and asked that Yemoja might bless him in his new endeavor.

Bode was silent throughout, until she tapped his shoulder gently and asked him to stand up. "You are free to go now. Learn to sow more with your thoughts and the fruits will

31

depend on the seed. You have Yemoja's blessing."

Hunger is not a bedfellow you want to write love letters to, or, heavens forbid, pray for, so he knew he had to do something. He had gone for the necessary bath and that is one thing he didn't want to remember either. His skin still hung indifferently on his bones but his cheeks were beginning to fill out. He took a critical look at his rump and wondered when the eczema would fade off. He wondered if she had noticed the ugly patches when she had washed him, and his face burned remembering with some shame that he had involuntarily been aroused.

For goodness sake, she is the frigging priestess. He wanted to know if she felt anything or was disgusted by his skeletal frame. His mother had given him one keen look and said nothing. He was not going to tell her anything. *But what would I have told her if she had asked? I had the bath and yes, mother, I was aroused by the frigging priestess, and yes, she acted like she didn't know if I was human.* He sighed and pulled on his shirt.

His new job was very tiring. He had to check on his junior staff who tended to take his instructions with a nonchalance that irritated him. He walked to the factory floor and met Modupe, his secretary, who considered him with amusement.

"The machines are down this morning and the computer boys don't seem to know what the problem is with the image transfer computer." She carried a flip chart close to her voluptuous breasts. He dragged his eyes away from her chest, frowning as he concentrated on the problem.

"Where is Francis?" he asked, looking around for the fellow.

Modupe shrugged and pointed in the general direction

of the computer room and stated mildly that she was sure Francis would be somewhere in the inner room, moved close, and thrust her flimsily covered breasts at him. She was chewing gum as usual.

Bode frowned, turned on his heels, and headed back. He felt the sweat trickle down his anus and made for the toilet next to his office, alarmed.

His picture of the priestess came again and he sighed in some despair, gradually wondering if she had placed a spell on him. He entered his office and opened a drawer, taking a generous swig of brandy to calm his jumping nerves. Modupe stood by the door watching him.

"Now what?" he snarled at her

"You are in some temper this morning so what is the problem?"

Bode imagined himself burying his head in those breasts, and mumbling the truth, and then swore violently, asking his secretary to get the hell out of his office that instant.

His secretary fled.

He sat at his desk and held his head in his hands, rocking himself in some unnamed and unrecognizable pain.

The office was silent and his thoughts were loud in his heart. She did not know my dream, so, when had the fascination with the body of the priestess taken over his thoughts?

Last market day he had visited his mother and watched the pleasure in her eyes when he gave her money and announced with pride that he would ensure she could expect that on a monthly basis.

He was happy until she gently asked him if he was thinking of settling down now. He told her he would do that when the time was right.

He knew the instant he saw the anxious expression on his mother's face, the secret she had been hiding. *Man, she thinks I can't get it up. She thinks maybe that is why I have avoided girls and not mentioned a coming bride nor shown interest in any of the village girls.* He was horrified. He looked at his mother and Bode saw the fear, the anxiety, and he was chagrinned. The knowledge they wordlessly shared at that moment was like a naked bride standing silently between them, untouched. Bode swallowed, muttered a goodbye, and hurried away.

Two days later, the image of the priestess when she washed him flashed into his mind—he had been aroused and had stayed that way ever since.

There was a knock on his door and he growled permission for the person to enter. Seconds later he was gasping in shock, desperately trying to draw in breath to a constricted throat, because in resplendent white with white gloves stood the priestess.

She smiled and walked further into the office.

He stared at her as he tried to swallow his salty saliva. *Have I conjured her up?*

She smiled and stretched out her hand for a handshake and he shuddered.

His voice was flat when he said, "Practicing spells in the open now are you?"

The priestess laughed and he was shocked to find the sound pleasing. His palms were sweaty. He cursed inwardly. *I didn't go to school, make the grade, and be jobless for eight years so that I can find a darned priestess attractive, did I?* Who was playing a trick on him, he wanted to know. He forced himself to listen to her.

"I am sure you have a reason to say what you just did,

but I am the doctor attached to the division here and I was asked to talk to you about your staff."

Bode stared in disbelief. "You are a doctor for real?"

"I am a traditionalist by religion but a doctor by profession. What seems to be the problem?"

He was still staring in shock wondering if he was dreaming but he watched her as she sat down, removed her gloves and presented him a letter which introduced her as Dr. Miss Oladunni.

He read the letter slowly and his inner equilibrium returned, so he became businesslike. He asked her what she wanted to know. They shared notes on some of the staff. She asked to have an office where she could talk to the staff. Working hours, if the staff had time given to them, to be involved in recreational activities, like darts or play scrabble.

Bode went through the conversation with half his mind noting small things like the fact that she had good nails, had them polished, and did not wear heavy perfume. He caught himself watching her curiously.

Minutes later the conversation was at an end and he casually asked her if she would like to walk round the premises. He explained that he was the production manager and he had the responsibility to watch the printing machines, determine billboards, and sometimes he had to supervise the copyists.

On their walk round the premises, the young male staff gave her admiring looks which she didn't seem to notice, and she had a small smile and a firm handshake for those she stopped by to say hello.

He returned to his office after a light lunch and was surprised that he was exhilarated. His secretary Modupe

35

was not impressed and had a scowl on her face.

The next day Modupe came to the office more skimpily clad than usual, causing Bode to call her into his office.

"Did you plan on coming to the office to work today"? he growled at her.

Modupe smiled and went over to sit close to his desk, crossing her legs. He saw more than he wanted and shoved her off his desk angrily.

In a voice that had gone cold and steely he demanded that she should go home and come back when she was more appropriately dressed and ready to work.

Modupe gave him one long look and decided to be bold. "I don't think I have a set of clothes different from what I am wearing. It does not affect my work."

Bode reached for his phone. "Hello, Mrs. Adedeji, could you find me a replacement secretary for tomorrow morning? My present secretary is on suspension as of this morning. In the meantime, please ask security to remove her from my office right now. I will be in the accounts office while that is affected. Thanks."

Modupe stared at him in shock, but he simply walked past her, out of the office. He had a job to do, and with Yemoja's blessing, he would do it.